This book belongs to Joseph Thompkins

D1395783

First published in hardback in Great Britain by
HarperCollins Publishers Ltd in 1999
3 5 7 9 10 8 6 4 2
First published in Picture Lions in 2000
1 3 5 7 9 10 8 6 4 2

Picture Lions is an imprint of the Children's Division,
part of HarperCollins Publishers Ltd.

ISBN: 0 00 198329 6 (Hardback)
ISBN: 0 00 664682 4 (Picture Lions)

Copyright © Nick Butterworth 1999
The author asserts the moral right to
be identified as the author of the work.

A CIP catalogue record for this title is
available from the British Library.
All rights reserved. No part of this
publication may be reproduced, stored
in a retrieval system or transmitted in
any form or by any means, electronic, mechanical,
photocopying, recording or otherwise,
without the prior permission of
HarperCollins Publishers Ltd,
77-85 Fulham Palace Road,
Hammersmith, London W6 8JB.

The HarperCollins website address is: www.fireandwater.com

Printed and bound in Singapore

PERCY'S BUMPY RIDE

NICK BUTTERWORTH

PictureLions

An Imprint of HarperCollinsPublishers

Percy the park keeper was hard at work. Bang! Bang! Bang! Bang! Squeak, squeak, squeak. Tap, tap, tappity-tap. Bang! Bang! Ouch!

For three whole days, sounds like these had been coming from Percy's workshop. What was he doing? Percy's friends, the animals who lived in the park, could only guess.

"I think he's making a bird table," said a squirrel.

"It could be a park bench," said a rabbit.

"It might be a . . ." But nobody heard what the hedgehog thought it might be.

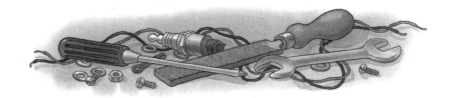

At that moment, there came the roar of an engine. The workshop doors burst open and above the noise of the engine, they heard Percy's voice.

"Make way! Make way!"
With a great clanking sound and a lot of smoke, Percy emerged from the workshop sitting on top of a very strange machine.

Percy pushed a switch and the engine coughed and spluttered into silence.

"Well," said Percy, "what do you think?"

"I know what I think," said the fox. "I think, *what is it?*"

"This is my new lawn mower," said Percy, patting the machine. "I've got terribly behind with cutting the grass. My old mower is so slow. But with this, I'll just fly around the park."

"Will it really fly?" asked the hedgehog.

"It's a lawn mower," chuckled Percy. "The propeller on top is to fan me with cool air while I'm mowing."

Percy turned a key and the engine clanked into life again.

"Come on," he said. "Let's try it out. All aboard!"

With everyone sitting on his new mower, Percy began to chug across the grass. "It works!" shouted Percy as he admired the stripe of closely cut grass behind the mower. "Let's try it a bit faster."

Percy pushed a lever. But what happened
next took everyone by surprise.

The engine roared and the propeller whirled faster and faster. Then, to everyone's astonishment, Percy's mower began to lift into the air.

"It does fly!" squealed the hedgehog. "You're so clever, Percy!"

"Er, well, I wouldn't say that," said Percy as he struggled with the mower's controls. He was beginning to think that the propeller was not such a good idea.

At first, the flying mower seemed to
be deciding all by itself where to go.
But after a while, Percy found that by
pushing and pulling levers he could
make the mower go where he
wanted.

For the animals it was very exciting.
Only the ducks and the owl had ever
been this high up in the air before.

mower climbed high into the sky, the animals were amazed by what they could see below them.

Suddenly the badger called out.
"Tree ahead, Percy!"
"Oh, er, thank you," said Percy.
He pulled hard on a lever and just managed to swoop over the tall tree, mowing some leaves as he passed.

"Look at those sheep," said one of the rabbits. "They've made a shape like a hand. I think they're waving to us."

Suddenly the badger called out. "Tree ahead, Percy!"
"Oh, er, thank you," said Percy.
He pulled hard on a lever and just managed to swoop over the tall tree, mowing some leaves as he passed.

As the mower climbed high into the sky, the animals were amazed by what they could see below them.

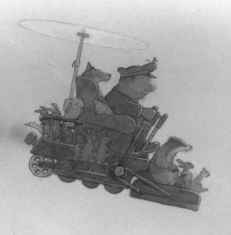

"Look at those sheep," said one of the
rabbits. "They've made a shape like
a hand. I think they're waving to us."

"I doubt it," said Percy. "I shouldn't think they've even noticed us."

"I think they have noticed us," said the rabbit. "Look!"

The sheep had now arranged themselves into the shape of a face. It looked very much like a face they all knew.

Everyone waved to the sheep.

Percy wished he could join them. He didn't realise how quickly his wish would be granted.

Whether the spinning propeller on
top of the mower had begun to feel
giddy, or whether it had just had enough of
turning round and round, no one could be
sure. But suddenly, it stopped. And just as
suddenly, so did the mower's engine.

"That's better," said the fox. "It's nice and quiet."

"It's quiet," said Percy, "but it's not nice. We're going to crash!"

Down went the mower and down went the mower's passengers.

"It's such a pity you don't have wings," said the owl.

"Isn't it!" said Percy, as he shot past her.

The sheep below looked worried.
They began to run all over the field.
"Get out of the way!" shouted Percy.
But the sheep didn't. Instead, they huddled together, right under where Percy and the animals were falling.
Then Percy realised what the sheep were doing.

Now, instead of the hard ground below
him, Percy looked down to see a soft,
springy, woolly blanket.

The badger was the first to land. As each
one landed, they bounced on the soft,
woolly backs of the sheep.

E ven Percy, the heaviest of all, bounced
three times and was safely down.

Everyone said a big thank you to the sheep. They laughed and said they were very glad to help. They were only sorry they couldn't save Percy's mower.

Percy looked to where the mower had crash-landed in a tree.

"I won't be using that again," he said.

"What will you do?" said the hedgehog. "The grass in the park is still very long."

Percy sighed and scratched his head. Then he began to smile.

"Er . . . sheep," said Percy. "How would you like to visit a field of lovely, long, tasty, green grass . . ?"